MUSIC USE NOTE

Licensees are solely responsible for obtaining formal written permission from copyright owners to use copyrighted music in the performance of this play and are strongly cautioned to do so. If no such permission is obtained by the licensee, then the licensee must use only original music that the licensee owns and controls. Licensees are solely responsible and liable for all music clearances and shall indemnify the copyright owners of the play(s) and their licensing agent, Samuel French, against any costs, expenses, losses and liabilities arising from the use of music by licensees. Please contact the appropriate music licensing authority in your territory for the rights to any incidental music.

IMPORTANT BILLING AND CREDIT REQUIREMENTS

If you have obtained performance rights to this title, please refer to your licensing agreement for important billing and credit requirements.

G000126568

OUTSIDE PEOPLE was originally produced by Vineyard Theatre and Naked Angels in New York City on December 21st, 2012. The performance was directed by Evan Cabnet, with sets by Takeshi Kata, costumes by Jessica Wegener Shay, lighting by Ben Stanton, and sound by Bill BC Du Boff. The Production Stage Manager was Charles M. Turner III. The cast was as follows:

MALCOLM. . . . . Matt Dellapina

XIAO MEI . . . . Li Jun Li

DA WEI "DAVID" WANG . . . . Nelson Lee

SAMANYA . . . . .Sonequa Martin-Green

CHARACTERS

MALCOLM – 20s

XIAO MEI – 20s

DA WEI "DAVID" WANG – 20s

SAMANYA – 20s

SETTING

Beijing, PRC

TIME

Present

AUTHOR'S NOTES

Some of the dialogue is in pinyin, a romanization of Mandarin characters. In the script, English translations are given in brackets, but in performance there should be no supertitles or other assistance for the English-speaking audience.

For Rachel

SCENE 1

(A private room in an upscale neon expat bar in Beijing.)

(Chinese hip-hop playing)

(A Chinese girl, **XIAO MEI,** *sits across from an American guy,* **MALCOLM**. *She's dressed up to go out; he wears jeans and a rumpled T-shirt, fresh off a transcontinental flight, uncomfortably aware of how he might look or smell.)*

(There are a bunch of empty Yanjing beer bottles on the table and two unoccupied chairs, draped with a purse and jacket.)

(The song ends, and there's a long, awkward pause.)

*(***MALCOLM*** and* **XIAO MEI** *glance at one another.)*

(He shrugs, laughs. She smiles.)

XIAO MEI. Sorry, my English…

MALCOLM. It's okay. My fault. My Chinese should be way better than it is by now. Really. Duì bu qǐ…Wǒ de zhōng guó. *[Sorry…for my China.]*

XIAO MEI. Méi shì. *[No problem.]*

(They both look around, hoping to be rescued.)

(An American pop song starts to play.)

MALCOLM. Um, so…

XIAO MEI. Hm?

MALCOLM. *(pointing to the speakers)* Bon Jovi.

XIAO MEI. Yes…?

MALCOLM. I used to – in fifth grade? Like – *"Slippery When Wet"*? I thought was like…

(He can't explain. Gives up.)

XIAO MEI. *(doesn't get it)* So how – do you meet Dà Wéi?

MALCOLM. Oh, Wang? *(The way he pronounces it rhymes with "bang".)* We were roommates. In college. We lived together?

XIAO MEI. Ah.

MALCOLM. I mean – I don't know if that came out – um. "Lived together" as in we were placed in a room. Via lottery. Nothing – romantic, or anything. Tā shì wǒde péngyou *[He is my friend.]* is all...friends?

(She smiles politely.)

XIAO MEI. Duì le. Wǒ tīng dǒng le. *[Yeah. I understand.]*

MALCOLM. Nǐ ne? *[And you?]* How did you – um...

(He takes out a little red Chinese/English dictionary, flips through it.)

MALCOLM. Shit. Sorry...

(XIAO MEI *looks around, waiting.)*

Nǐ shì zěnme rènshi...? *[How do you know...?]* Fuck.

(DAVID *and* **SAMANYA** *enter from the bar, laughing.* **DAVID** *is Chinese,* **SAMANYA** *from Cameroon. They are both beautiful, expensively dressed, and speak fluent English and Mandarin.)*

(DAVID *is balancing a bottle of liquor in one hand and four glasses in the other.)*

(He shuts the door, blocking out the music.)

DAVID. Hey – sorry about that, guys. Bartender's a bit overwhelmed in there...*(He sets it all down on the table.)* But it was worth the wait, uh? Wǒ men dài lǐwù lái le! *[We come bearing gifts!]*

(pours out four drinks, sloppily)

Gān bēi *[Cheers]*, motherfuckers!

SAMANYA. Gān bēi!

XIAO MEI. Gān bēi.

Outside People

Zayd Dohrn

A SAMUEL FRENCH ACTING EDITION

SAMUEL
FRENCH

FOUNDED 1830

SAMUELFRENCH.COM
SAMUELFRENCH-LONDON.CO.UK

FOR PRODUCTION ENQUIRIES

UNITED STATES AND CANADA
Info@SamuelFrench.com
1-866-598-8449

UNITED KINGDOM AND EUROPE
Theatre@SamuelFrench-London.co.uk
020-7255-4302

Each title is subject to availability from Samuel French, depending upon
country of performance. Please be aware that OUTSIDE PEOPLE may
not be licensed by Samuel French in your territory. Professional and
amateur producers should contact the nearest Samuel French office or
licensing partner to verify availability.

(They all slug their shots, except **MALCOLM**.*)*

MALCOLM. *(catching on)* Oh. Sorry. Guan bay…

(He drinks his. They all watch him. He coughs.)

MALCOLM. Hahhh…

SAMANYA. You all right?

DAVID. *(laughing)* Don't hurt yourself now. Your first night.

MALCOLM. Uch – what the fuck?!?!

DAVID. *(refilling the glasses)* It's *erguotou,* man. Chinese fire liquor. Made from – sorghum grass or something. Hundred-twenty proof. For toasting special occasions…

MALCOLM. I'm honored.

SAMANYA. It's Xiao Mei's birthday.

MALCOLM. Oh, sorry. Can you tell her – "Happy Birthday" for me?

DAVID. It's more polite if you look at her when you talk.

MALCOLM. Happy. Birthday.

XIAO MEI. Thank. You.

MALCOLM. I feel like we should be speaking Chinese though…if I'm the only one here who doesn't –

DAVID. She understands a lot, don't worry.

MALCOLM. Yeah, but I should at least try. Feel like I'm confirming every stereotype of a provincial American redneck, with my –

DAVID. You are. With that outfit.

MALCOLM. Why? What's wrong with my –

DAVID. You look like a blind hobo, Malcolm. Make an effort. This isn't Africa, y'know. We do have running water here.

SAMANYA. We have running water in Africa, shǎ bī. *[stupid cunt]*

MALCOLM. I wanted to take a shower at the hotel, remember? You were the one who said we had no time to –

SAMANYA. I think he looks kinda cute and cuddly, actually.

DAVID. Oh yeah?

SAMANYA. You should try it some time, Dave. Relax. Dress it down a bit.

DAVID. No thank you. Chinese guy dresses like that, looks like he's about to deliver some moo shu pork.

SAMANYA. Well deliver then, bitch! I'm hungry!

(they laugh)

DAVID. *(raising a glass)* Hey – to Malcolm's long-awaited arrival in Beijing, uh? Huānyíng wài guó de guìbīn. Gān bēi! *[Welcome honored foreign guest. Cheers!]*

ALL. Gān bēi!

(They drink again. MALCOLM almost hacks up a lung.)

MALCOLM. Ach. Sorry…I'm sorry. I haven't eaten anything but peanuts in like – eighteen hours…

SAMANYA. What're you doing here again?

DAVID. I told you, he's come to work for me.

MALCOLM. No. No, we're talking about that, as a possibility, Wang. I'm just – visiting, for the moment. Didn't have much going on in the States, so…

SAMANYA. You want to fā cái *[strike it rich]* like Dà Wéi, huh? Come to China and become a rich dà wàn er *[big shot]*?

MALCOLM. Um?

SAMANYA. "Big shot."

MALCOLM. Oh, ha. I don't think I'm actually constitutionally capable of that kind of –

DAVID. *(interrupting)* Hey – what were you guys talking about? Before we so rudely interrupted?

MALCOLM. Oh, I'm afraid I wasn't much of a –

XIAO MEI. Bon Jo-vi.

DAVID. No, God, Malcolm. Not Bon Jovi…*(to the girls)* When we were at Stanford, Malcolm used to blast Eighties hair bands and synth-pop like twenty-four hours a day. Prince. Erasure. Depeche Mode, like we were –

MALCOLM. Long time ago, Wang.

DAVID. Not really. Our whole suite thought the two of us were tóng xìng liàn *[homosexuals]*, I think, with all the –

MALCOLM. We were eighteen.

DAVID. And I guarantee if we go through your iTunes right now, it's at least ninety-five percent showtunes and glam rock. Am I wrong?

MALCOLM. Yes. Actually –

DAVID. Really?

MALCOLM. Yeah. Completely. In fact. *(glancing at* **SAMANYA***)* I have lots of um…hip-hop in there…

(**DAVID** *cackles.*)

DAVID. Okay, Tupac…

XIAO MEI. *(rescuing him)* I also like Era-sure.

DAVID. Oh, see? Well then. You guys have a lot in common, huh? Maybe you should get to know each other better. *Biblically…*

(an uncomfortable pause)

XIAO MEI. Bib-li-clee…?

MALCOLM. Nothing. Nothing, he's just being a –

(**DAVID** *slaps some money on the table.*)

DAVID. *(to* **SAMANYA***)* Here! Wanna grab us another bottle, qīn'ài de *[sweetheart]*?

SAMANYA. Sure. *(to* **XIAO MEI***)* Hey, come on – Let's go pee and let the men talk about us, hǎo bù hǎo? *[all right?]*

XIAO MEI. Hǎo de. *[Okay.]*

(**SAMANYA** *and* **XIAO MEI** *stand.*)

DAVID. Don't take too long.

SAMANYA. Mind your own business.

(The girls exit together, holding hands. **MALCOLM** *watches them go.)*

MALCOLM. Holding hands…

DAVID. Yeah. Friendly thing here. Guys do it too, hey – how're you feeling now? All right?

MALCOLM. Good. Yeah.

DAVID. You look like shit.

MALCOLM. I'm tired. And a little bit wasted. Take it easy on me.

DAVID. Seems like she's digging you though, uh? Not bad, your first night.

MALCOLM. Who is…?

DAVID. Who do you think? Xiao Mei.

MALCOLM. What? Nah.

DAVID. Definitely! She's feeling it. I can tell.

MALCOLM. How?

DAVID. How? Because she's giving off some major vibes! You can't feel the vibes?

MALCOLM. No, I can't – understand a single fucking thing that's happened so far, Wang, since I got here. "Vibes," or…I just want to go to bed. I think it's – *(checks his watch)* – noon in Brooklyn? I'm gonna die.

DAVID. Here. Have some pills. Help with the jet lag.

(He offers a little paper envelope.)

MALCOLM. What is it?

DAVID. Ground up cow scrotum or something. Traditional herbal remedy. Give you lots of macho energy.

MALCOLM. *(laughs)*

DAVID. Come on. I insist you take her back to your hotel tonight and ravish her like a true pale-skinned barbarian.

MALCOLM. She doesn't seem the type…

DAVID. The type? Show me the respect of assuming I know how to read signals here, man. Believe me. She's down!

MALCOLM. She's way out of my league…

DAVID. Yeah, but that's the best thing about being a lǎo wài *[foreigner]* here! You climb a step or two up the totem pole just from having a US passport. You rate a five in the States, you're at least like…a seven in Beijing.

MALCOLM. Well that's – flattering, I guess.

DAVID. Like bald Eurotrash in LA with the starlets in the convertible? That's you in China, man!

MALCOLM. Anyway, we can't even talk. It's so awkward. I wouldn't even know where to –

DAVID. I thought you studied Chinese at school.

MALCOLM. I did! For a year. But apparently it was actually – Pig Latin or something, because she didn't understand a thing I said. Not a word.

DAVID. Tones. Takes some time getting used to. You'll have biāo zhǔnde Běijīng huà *[nice sounding Beijing-speak]* in no time. Trust me. You know the best way to learn a new language, Malc? Pillow talk. That's why my Bantu has gotten so – *(He kisses the tips of his fingers.)*

MALCOLM. Samanya is really – stunning, by the way…

DAVID. Oh? Thanks.

MALCOLM. Look like 50 Cent over there…keep half-expecting you to break out a bottle of Cristal and start cutting up a kilo on the tabletop.

DAVID. Well, I would – I would, you know, but possession of narcotics is a capital offense in China, Malcolm, so – we'll stick to the *erguotou* and cow balls, huh? Gān bēi!

MALCOLM. Gān bēi –

*(**MALCOLM** swallows the contents of the envelope.)*

(They drink.)

*(**MALCOLM** coughs.)*

MALCOLM. Ah. Fuck…again.

DAVID. *(laughs)* Good to see you, man…Forgot what a lightweight you are.

MALCOLM. Yeah? You've changed a lot, Wang.

DAVID. You think?

MALCOLM. In a good way…

DAVID. Older?

MALCOLM. No. No, you look the same. Just –

DAVID. In my element.

MALCOLM. Yeah. Maybe…

DAVID. Hard to understand somebody until you see where he comes from, eh? You look the same too. Bit fatter.

MALCOLM. Thanks, man. For setting this all up. I really –

DAVID. Oh, it's nothing.

MALCOLM. It's not nothing. I needed it. A change of scenery…I wanted to let you know, I appreciate –

(The girls return to the table, **SAMANYA** *dancing and holding a new bottle.)*

SAMANYA. Heeeey! Miss us, ge menr? *[boys?]*

DAVID. Dāng rán. *[Of course.]* What took so long?

SAMANYA. Bartender was hitting on Xiao Mei. She told him to bì zuí *[shut up]* his wack-ass pickup line. I like this one, Dave! Nà me lì haì. *[Super hardcore.]* Where'd you find her?

DAVID. Around.

MALCOLM. *(to* **SAMANYA***)* Your Chinese is – amazing, by the way.

SAMANYA. Oh, thanks. I've been here since forever. My dad works in the Cameroonian embassy. So – I basically am Chinese, right? *(to* **XIAO MEI***)* Wǒ shì bù shì Zhōng guó rén? *[I'm Chinese, right?]*

XIAO MEI. Duì, xiàng gè lǎo Zhōng guó tōng. *[Yeah, she sounds like an old China hand.]*

SAMANYA. Went to Beijing elementary and everything.

DAVID. I can picture you. As a sixth grader. With the little blue Mao suit covering the crotchless panties from Milan…

SAMANYA. You know it.

XIAO MEI. *(a bit drunk)* "Beijing United." Bù shì Zhōng guó rén de xué xiào. Tā men kěn dìng bù chuān máo zhǔxí dē Zhōng Shān Zhuāng! *[That's not a Chinese school. And they definitely don't wear any Mao suits there!]*

(Everybody laughs except **MALCOLM***, who didn't quite catch it.)*

MALCOLM. What?

DAVID. She says Samanya went to this – international academy. Not authentic Beijing public school. She's a poser.

SAMANYA. You're the fucking poser, "Dave." I'm way more Chinese than you are.

DAVID. You think so?

SAMANYA. Hell yeah. Xiao Mei, who's more Chinese? Me or Dà Wéi.

XIAO MEI. *(without hesitation)* Dà Wéi.

DAVID. *(laughs)*

SAMANYA. Bitch! I was just starting to like you!

XIAO MEI. Dà Wéi is very Chinese. Wú lùn tā zěnmā xiǎng, tā zǒng huì shì yǐ zì wǒ wéi zhōng xīn. *[Even though he doesn't really want to be, he can't erase this true part of himself.]*

SAMANYA. *(laughing)* Oh shit!

MALCOLM. What? What'd she say?

DAVID. Nothing. Ignore her. Little Red Guard propaganda slogans.

SAMANYA. No, she thinks Dave's a traitor. He's hurt the feelings of the Chinese people by becoming so – westernized.

DAVID. She's just jealous 'cause she never got to go overseas.

SAMANYA. Well, she didn't have your guānxi *[connections]*, right?

DAVID. Or my test scores.

MALCOLM. "Guānxi"?

SAMANYA. Connections.

MALCOLM. Ah.

DAVID. You think guānxi got me into Stanford, Sam?

SAMANYA. Didn't hurt, Dave. At least got you your student visa, no?

(beat)

DAVID. Well, that's true…here, to Uncle Feng, eh? And his NPC post. Gān bēi!

ALL. Gān bēi!

(They all drink again.)

SAMANYA. Hey – You said you had a good story, right? Tell.

DAVID. Oh, yeah – Okay. So. Check this out, Malc. Guess where I spent yesterday afternoon?

MALCOLM. Where?

DAVID. Police department. Character witness.

SAMANYA. For who?

DAVID. A friend.

SAMANYA. You don't have any friends. Or character.

DAVID. Kind of a dirty story anyway. Not so suitable for female friends…maybe I'll tell Malcolm later.

SAMANYA. *(laughing)* Asshole – tell! Nǐ shuō de shì shuí? *[Who are you talking about?]* One of your other girlfriends?

DAVID. One of our janitors, actually. Mister Zhang? All right, so. We had this American lǎo wài *[foreign]* accountant with us last week. Doing the books, right? Blonde lady from Texas. "Barbara."

SAMANYA. Get to the dirty bits.

DAVID. Okay, so. Barbara's in the ladies room Tuesday morning. From what I understand. In the stall, minding her own business. Suddenly Mister Zhang busts in on her. Middle of her pee!

*(He grabs **SAMANYA**'s knees, spreads her legs apart. She squeals, bats him away.)*

So. She screams. Like that. Thinking he's about to… have his wicked Oriental way with her. Guards come running. And when they get there, Mister Zhang is already on his hands and knees. *Kao tao*-ing on the bathroom floor. Apologizing for his rude behavior. Police take him in for questioning, and he confesses right away: "I'm very sorry, officers. I don't mean to offend the kind Miss. I just have to know – does the foreigner's máo *[body hair]* match her tóufa *[head hair]*?" *(for* **MALCOLM***'s benefit:)* "Does the rug match the drapes?"

SAMANYA. *(laughs)* Man, your English is good…

DAVID. *(cocky)* It is, right?

XIAO MEI. Wǒ bù xǐ huan nǐ zhè ge gùshì. Gào sù tā bù hé shì. *[I don't think this is a very nice story to tell your friend.]*

MALCOLM. He wasn't trying to rape her or –

DAVID. No. No, see – the cops want to cut off his balls or something. But he was just curious about foreign girls! This is what comes from a national policy of sexual repression, Malcolm. Ten, fifteen years ago, Chinese people are still being taught to love only the State, right? Beijing women wearing shapeless blue potato sacks to work, look like fucking Jackie Chan. Now, all of a sudden – *(indicating* **XIAO MEI***)* – Chinese girls are decked out in the Louis Vuitton! Prada. Mini-skirts, *thongs.* Whole nation popped one big collectivist boner, all at the same time. People don't know what to do with these feelings. It's overwhelming. Which is why a nice guy like Mister Zhang can be literally driven insane by the mystery of blonde bush!

*(***SAMANYA*** laughs.)*

*(***DAVID*** glances at* **MALCOLM***, who is slowly nodding off.)*

DAVID. Hey – Guìbīn! *[VIP!]* We boring you?

MALCOLM. *(starting up)* Uh? What?

(They all laugh.)

MALCOLM. Sorry – no, I'm just really – *(He slugs his drink.)* Okay? Gān bēi…

(He puts his head down on the table.)

DAVID. Why didn't you sleep on the plane, motherfucker? I told you –

MALCOLM. I tried. But there was this – really fat guy sitting next to me? Overflowing his armrest –

XIAO MEI. Americans are very fat.

DAVID. Should have let me upgrade you.

MALCOLM. No, it was fine. I don't want to be –

DAVID. Got a zillion miles banked. What am I supposed to do with 'em if not fix up my boy?

MALCOLM. It's fine. I don't like flying business anyway –

SAMANYA. Why not?

DAVID. Because. Malcolm took "Intro to Marxism" in college and now he thinks he's a communist. Spent the last five years bumming around the U.S., growing a beard like Che Guevara. Living in his car and making a documentary about like – vegan goat herders or something.

MALCOLM. *(overlapping)* Subsistence farmers.

DAVID. I only got him to come to China because he thinks we're still Socialists here. So now he gets all self-righteous when you try to talk to him about *business.*

MALCOLM. No. No, that's not – it's not a political statement, just –

XIAO MEI. I think Mal-colm have correct feeling about this...

MALCOLM. Oh. Thanks.

DAVID. Yeah, whatever. You can't talk to a Chinese about economics. She was brought up on Party propaganda. Probably never even been on an airplane before. And she actually believes in the sì xiàng jībĕn yuánzé *[Four Cardinal Principles]*, so –

XIAO MEI. No, this is not why, Dà Wéi...

DAVID. It is why.

XIAO MEI. Bùnéng shuō dàjiā zài jīngjì shàng dū yīnggāi píngdĕng. Shēng yì jìng zhēng ma, yĕ zhòng yào, dànshi mĕi gèrén dōu yīnggāi yŏu zuì jībĕn de rénquán hé réngé. Nĭ shuō bù duì ma? *[It's not that everyone should be economically equal. I understand the need for* *competition and business interests. But everyone should have some kind of basic human rights and dignity too, don't you think so?]*

DAVID. Eh – nǐ yào ràng wǒ diū miànzi mā? Zài wǒ péngyou dē miàn qián? *[Hey – You want to make me lose face? In front of my friend?]*

XIAO MEI. *(to* **MALCOLM***)* Sorry. I don't mean –

*(***MALCOLM** *doesn't respond. He has fallen asleep at the table.)*

DAVID. Ah. Poor fucker. Nǐ sòng tā huí "St. Regis" bīn guǎn, xíng ma? *[You'll help him get back to the St. Regis hotel, huh?]*

XIAO MEI. Méi wèn tí. *[No problem.]*

DAVID. Good. I have to pee. Come on, yáng guǐzi *[foreign devil]*, you can hold it for me.

SAMANYA. Sure, let me just get out my miniature chopsticks...

*(***DAVID** *laughs, staggers out of the bar.)*

*(***SAMANYA** *hesitates.)*

SAMANYA. Hey, Xiao Mei – *(rummaging through her purse)* Listen, I was thinking maybe – we could get together sometime, you know? Hang out, or –

(She offers **XIAO MEI** *her card.)*

XIAO MEI. *(taking it with both hands)* Nà tài hǎo le. *[That'd be great.]*

SAMANYA. Yeah? Cool. I'd love it. Really. Xiǎo xīn yī diǎn, uh? *[Be careful, huh?]*

(She exits after **DAVID***.)*

*(***XIAO MEI** *looks at* **MALCOLM***, who is fast asleep with his head on the table, snoring softly.)*

(She taps him gently on the shoulder.)

XIAO MEI. Hm – excuse me...Mal-colm...? Hello?

(He opens his eyes, sees her.)

SCENE 2

(**MALCOLM**'s *hotel room*)

(*The lights are off. An unzipped duffel lies on the floor next to the bed – he hasn't yet unpacked.*)

(*On the bedside table are several bottles of prescription medication, a Beijing guidebook, some U.S. dollars.*)

(*The sound of a keycard in the lock outside, and the door opens.*)

(**MALCOLM** *and* **XIAO MEI** *enter, both a bit wasted.*)

(*He gropes blindly for the switch, turns on the lights.*)

MALCOLM. Here we are…

XIAO MEI. Hǎo de. *[Great].*

(*She takes off her shoes, using him for balance.*)

MALCOLM. Um…you want something to drink, Xiao Mei? We got uh – (*He opens the fridge.*) Standard mini-bar fare…

(*showing her*)

Jack Daniels? Tanqueray?

XIAO MEI. Bùyòng xiè. *[No thanks.]* I am – too drunk already.

MALCOLM. Oh. Me too. Yeah. How 'bout – uh. Kě kǒu kě lè *[Coca-cola]*?

XIAO MEI. No…

MALCOLM. Sprite? How do you say in…?

XIAO MEI. Xuě bì. *[Sprite]*

MALCOLM. Xuě bì.

XIAO MEI. Bù shì "bí". *[Not "bi".]* Fourth tone.

MALCOLM. Bì.

XIAO MEI. (*laughs*) Oh. No – this is – very bad word the way you say, Mal-colm.

MALCOLM. Really? Wow. Sorry. You want a – Sprite…?

XIAO MEI. No. Xiè xie. *[Thanks.]*

MALCOLM. Okay. My bad. *(He closes the fridge.)* My Chinese…

XIAO MEI. Méi shì. *[It's fine.]*

MALCOLM. Bù hǎo yìsi. *[I'm embarrassed.]* I have to –

XIAO MEI. Hm?

MALCOLM. Um…I gotta – Y'know.

(He gestures toward the bathroom, mimes peeing.)

(She laughs, covering her mouth with her hand.)

XIAO MEI. Xíng. Qù ba. Méi shì. *[Okay. Go ahead. It's fine.]*

(He goes into the bathroom and shuts the door.)

(XIAO MEI looks around the room, wanders over to the closet, checks her lipstick in the mirror.)

(She picks up one of the prescription bottles on the bedside table, looks at it curiously.)

(MALCOLM's voice comes through the bathroom door, singing drunkenly.)

MALCOLM. *(offstage)* Oh-oh – Make it I swea-ar…Whoa-oh – Livin' on a prayer…*

(XIAO MEI laughs to herself, not covering her mouth this time.)

(The sound of the toilet flushing. Water running in the sink.)

(XIAO MEI puts down the pill bottle.)

(MALCOLM comes out of the bathroom, a bit unsteady.)

MALCOLM. Hey – Sorry.

XIAO MEI. *(gesturing at the bottles)* So many medicine.

MALCOLM. *(crossing to her)* Oh. Yeah, I know.

XIAO MEI. *(reading a label)* "Shan-ash"?

MALCOLM. Xanax. It's a – anti-anxiety…I get – nervous sometimes? Around people? No big deal. I can handle it, pretty much, just –

---

*See Music Use Note on page 3

XIAO MEI. *(another label)* "Wal-tresh"?

(MALCOLM opens the drawer of the bedside table, sweeps the pill bottles inside, closes the drawer.)

MALCOLM. It's ridiculous, I know. Take more pills than my hypochondriac grandmother...Wŏ shì lǎo tóu. *[I'm an old fart.]*

XIAO MEI. Ah! Very good Chinese!

MALCOLM. Yeah. Speak better when I'm drunk. Remember more words, y'know? Fewer inhibitions...or whatever.

(beat)

(She looks around, biting her lip, waiting for him to make a move.)

(when he doesn't)

XIAO MEI. I will put on some mu-sic now, hǎo bù hǎo? *[okay?]*

MALCOLM. Oh, I don't have a stereo, but...

(She turns on the TV, finds a cheesy Hong Kong music video channel.)

(An Asian boy band is singing a romantic ballad.)

XIAO MEI. O-kay?

MALCOLM. Great, yeah.

(She sits on the bed, bounces a little.)

(He sits next to her.)

(They both laugh nervously.)

Thanks. By the way...for coming out, Xiao Mei. My first night. On your birthday and everything. Makes me feel really welcome, and –

(She kisses him.)

Wow.

(They kiss again. She starts to take off his shirt.)

MALCOLM. *(cont.)* Mm...Okay.

XIAO MEI. Wǒ de tiān! Zhēn duō máo! *[Oh my God! Lots of hair!]*

MALCOLM. What? Máo?

(She tugs on his chest hair.)

XIAO MEI. Nà me duō! *[So much!]* Lot of this.

MALCOLM. The hair? Yeah, I know. Sorry...it's a Jew thing, you know. Even my mom is like –

XIAO MEI. You are Jew?

MALCOLM. Me? Yeah...

XIAO MEI. Jew are very smart.

MALCOLM. Oh. Thanks. Smart, cheap, and hairy.

(She doesn't get it.)

XIAO MEI. Chinese man máo zhēn shǎo. *[have very little hair.]*

MALCOLM. Mm. Sorry. I didn't catch –

XIAO MEI. Suàn lē ba. *[Never mind.]*

(They kiss.)

(She starts to unbutton his pants. His passport belt is in the way.)

MALCOLM. Oops. Sorry.

(He unbuckles the belt, drops it on the floor.)

(She unzips his fly.)

Whoa. Wait – hold up a second...sorry.

XIAO MEI. Zěn me le? *[What's wrong?]*

MALCOLM. I uh – have something – I hafta tell you first, Xiao Mei, if that's – uh. Wǒ...gàosu...shìqíng...? *[I... tell you...thing...?]*

XIAO MEI. O-kay?

(He stands up, takes a deep breath.)

(She watches him.)

MALCOLM. Sorry. Don't mean to ruin the moment. Too late. *(laughs nervously)* It's a bit awkward, I know…if this were the States, it'd probably be a bit easier to – I'm pretty much a verbal person, I think, and uh…

(He paces.)

MALCOLM. *(cont.)* See, thing is, Xiao Mei – You seem really great to me…you know? But if we're about to do – what I think we were about to do? Which I would love to do? I have to tell you something first. If that's –

(He takes a deep breath.)

So. I think it's pretty obvious at this point that I'm not much of a "player"? Right? I mean I've only been with – a couple people. In college. And one time after…but apparently, one of those four "lucky ladies," unbeknownst to me, she had – this problem? You know? This issue…? Uh – Herpes?

(another deep breath)

I'm not supposed to be – contagious. If that makes any difference. I'm on medication. It's in remission. There are no open sores or – which is completely disgusting, I realize, to say "sores." But there's very little chance of your getting it from me, is all I'm trying to – and I'd still – like to be friends, or…

(beat)

XIAO MEI. I – sorry, Mal-colm. Some of this I can no –

MALCOLM. All right, yeah. I'll boil it down for you, all right? I have…herpes.

(He winces.)

XIAO MEI. Her piece?

MALCOLM. Ha…

(He takes out his Chinese-English dictionary, flips through it.)

(He can't find the word.)

Nope. I can't – shit…

XIAO MEI. I think I will – *(starting to leave)* Sorry, if I am –

MALCOLM No no no no, it.'s not you. It's not you, just –

(beat)

Can you hang on one sec?

(He fishes in his pocket for a business card. Picks up the hotel phone, dials, waits.)

Hey – it's me, man. It's Malcolm…yeah, sorry. I know. I got a second wind…she's – here, but – Hey, Samanya… no, I just wondered if you could translate something for me real quick, Wang? Sorry to be – I just need you to tell her about my…issue? If you could explain – right. And hopefully say it in such a way that it's not a complete deal breaker? Because I'd really like to – I mean I think she's super cool and…okay, thanks, man. Sorry to be calling so late, I –

(He hands the phone to **XIAO MEI.***)*

XIAO MEI. Wèi? *[Yes?]*

(She listens.)

XIAO MEI. Unh…unh…

*(***MALCOLM** *watches her.)*

Unh…unh…? Unh…

(beat)

Xíng. Wǒ tīng dǒng le. Zài jiàn. *[Okay. I understand. Bye.]*

(She hangs up the phone.)

MALCOLM. You got all that? Nǐ tīng de dǒng? *[Understand?]*

XIAO MEI. Duì. *[Yeah.]*

MALCOLM. I'm really…sorry, Xiao Mei, I –

XIAO MEI. Méi shì. *[It's nothing.]* I can – understand this, Mal-colm. I think. Happy that you tell me now.

MALCOLM. You are? Good, 'cause I thought it'd be – just to say it out loud, so…and if you don't want to do anything, now, that's cool. I'd understand why –

XIAO MEI. Mal-colm?

MALCOLM. Yes?

XIAO MEI. I am like this also, you know.

MALCOLM. What?

XIAO MEI. I am also like –

MALCOLM. You are…?

XIAO MEI. Duì. *[Yeah.]* The similar situation.

MALCOLM. You're kidding. Really?

(beat)

Does Wang know?

XIAO MEI. Mm. Yes, he know this about me I think…

MALCOLM. *(confused)* Wow. Is that why he figured we'd – get along or whatever? That we had this in common, or…?

XIAO MEI. Maybe?

MALCOLM. Huh. That's – wow, I mean that's really…great, Xiao Mei. Smart of him. In terms of…y'know, I know it can be – really tough to meet people in this – with this type of situation.

XIAO MEI. Yes.

MALCOLM. Yeah. So…it's been a really – long time for me…All right? Just so you know. If I'm not like – up to snuff or whatever, in terms of your expectations… for anything – that lasts longer than thirty-five seconds, or…

(She holds his face, looks into his eyes.)

(He's surprised at first, tries to look away, but she keeps him there.)

(They look at each other.)

MALCOLM. Okay…Yeah.

(They kiss, and she pulls him back onto the bed.)

SCENE 3

(The hotel room)

(Grey Beijing dawn seeps around the edges of the window curtains. The sounds of early morning traffic.)

(MALCOLM *lies across the comforter on the bed, in his underwear, asleep.)*

(The bathroom door opens silently, and **XIAO MEI** *enters, fully dressed, her hair wet from the shower.)*

(She tiptoes around the room, hunting for something.)

(She looks under **MALCOLM**'s *passport belt.)*

(Suddenly, there's a loud knock from outside. She freezes.)

(MALCOLM *stirs, opens his eyes, sees her)*

(another knock, more insistent this time)

(She puts down the belt.)

MALCOLM. Hello…?

DAVID. *(offstage)* Malc? Wake up, man! It's me –

MALCOLM. Oh. Hey –

DAVID. *(offstage)* Open the fucking door.

(MALCOLM *rolls out of bed, falls on the floor, pulls on his jeans)*

MALCOLM. 'kay…Hold on a sec…? *(whispering)* Sorry. I didn't know he'd be –

(XIAO MEI *shrugs –* "What can you do?")

(MALCOLM *tries to make the bed. It's a lost cause. He gives up, pulls on his shirt.)*

(DAVID *knocks again.)*

Okay! One second…

(XIAO MEI *opens the door)*

(*DAVID enters, wearing a different suit, carrying a cardboard tray with three Starbucks cups and a brown paper bag.*)

(*He takes in the room with a glance.*)

DAVID. Morning, all...

MALCOLM. Hey –

DAVID. (*to* **XIAO MEI***)* Nǐ zhēn kuài. *[You work fast.]*

XIAO MEI. Měi yǒu nǐ nèm mā kuài. *[Not as fast as you.]*

DAVID. I brought coffee. Muffins.

MALCOLM. Thanks.

DAVID. Méi shì. *[No problem.]* Everybody sleep well?

XIAO MEI. Nà wǒ xiān zóu lē. *[I should go.]*

(*she puts on her shoes*)

(*While her back is turned,* **DAVID** *takes a pen from his pocket, snags her underwear from where they've fallen underneath the bed, and holds them out to her.*)

DAVID. Don't forget your nèi kù, Xiǎo jiě *[panties, Miss].* Kind of breezy outside...

(*She takes them, looks him in the eye, puts them on under her skirt.*)

XIAO MEI. Xiè xie nǐ *[Thank you],* Dà Wéi. (*to* **MALCOLM***)* So it is – nice to meet you, Mal-colm. I will – see you some later time, maybe, okay?

MALCOLM. Oh. I – wǒ...hěn...*[I...really...]* Sorry. Zuó tiān...Hǎo wán...*[Yesterday...Fun...]*

DAVID. God, you sound like a fucking retard, you know that?

MALCOLM. Yes, I am aware of the problem, Wang. Thanks. (*to* **XIAO MEI***)* Duì bù qǐ...*[Sorry.]*

XIAO MEI. Méi guān xì. *[It's okay.]*

MALCOLM. Wǒ...xī wàng...*[I...hope...]* Uh. Xang – Xiǎng...? *[Want...?]* No.

DAVID. Jesus Christ. Who does Stanford have teaching Chinese these days, deaf-mutes? Xiao Mei – nǐ yào bù yào gōng zuò? *[You want the job or not?]*

XIAO MEI. Shénme? *[What?]*

DAVID. Yībǎi wǔshí kuài yīgè xiǎoshí, zěnme yàng? Jiāo zhège lǎowài shuō biāo zhǔnde pǔtōnghuà. *[How about a hundred fifty an hour? Teaching this old foreigner how to talk standard speak?]*

(XIAO MEI glances at MALCOLM)

XIAO MEI. Liǎng bǎi sān shí wǔ. *[Two thirty five.]*

DAVID. Liǎng bǎi. Wǒ yào tā dào chūntiān yǐqián jiù néng shuō de liúlì, hǎo bù hǎo? *[Two hundred. And I want him fluent by Spring, all right?]*

(beat)

XIAO MEI. Xíng. *[Okay.]*

DAVID. Good. Twice a week, after work. Chinese lessons. Here in the hotel. How's that sound?

MALCOLM. Really?

DAVID. Yeah, we'll have you up to speed in no time. Pay her two hundred rénmínbì *[people's currency]* per session. Cool?

MALCOLM. *(reaching for his money belt)* Now?

DAVID. No, not now. She's not a fucking drug dealer, Malcolm. After the lesson.

MALCOLM. Oh. Okay. Xiè xie *[thanks]*, Xiao Mei. That's really –

XIAO MEI. Bù kè qì. *[You're welcome.]*

MALCOLM. *(to DAVID)* How much is…?

DAVID. Twenty nine. Thirty bucks. Don't worry, I'll pay.

MALCOLM. No. No, I just – *(whispering)* I thought maybe we should pay her more.

DAVID. *(mock whispering)* No, we should not pay her more. I just bargained her down from two-thirty-five.

MALCOLM. What? Why?

DAVID. Because. That's how it works here, man. You negotiate.

MALCOLM. But – I don't care about an extra…six bucks, Wang. Jesus.

XIAO MEI. Méi shì, méi shì – *[It's fine – It's fine –]*

DAVID. What are you, UNICEF? Two hundred is what it costs. You want to insult her by paying extra like she's some kind of third world refugee?

XIAO MEI. No problem, Mal-colm, o-kay? Suàn le ba. *[Forget it.]*

MALCOLM. Okay. Sorry. Um. Míngtiān…wǒ…xī wàng…xué Zhōng guó. *[Tomorrow…I…Look forward…to learning of the China.]*

(**XIAO MEI** *smiles*)

XIAO MEI. Okay. Bye-bye.

(*she exits, shutting the door softly behind her*)

DAVID. So. That went pretty well, uh?

MALCOLM. Jesus Christ, Wang! What the fuck?

DAVID. What?

MALCOLM. Why'd you have to be such a – you made her feel like – we just had this *encounter* here, y'know, and I'm trying to be –

DAVID. She's fine, Malcolm. Trust me. Chinese girls are very practical in this regard. She doesn't expect your – American-style romance. Like in the movies. She's happy to get the work.

MALCOLM. "Like in the movies"? This from the guy who wept openly during *Titanic*?

DAVID. (*laughs*) Yeah, that's why I don't date Chinese girls anymore! After five years in the States. I like someone with a bit more – Hollywood in her.

MALCOLM. Anyway. I don't think you know what you're talking about. Xiao Mei doesn't seem "practical" to me. At all. In fact she's actually really –

DAVID. Different?

MALCOLM. From…?

DAVID. What you're used to.

MALCOLM. I don't think I'm "used to" anything except – sleeping alone in the backseat of my Honda with a camcorder and an empty pizza box on my chest, so –

DAVID. Different from girls you've had before.

MALCOLM. I guess…

DAVID. You know Westerners used to think Chinese women had sideways vaginas?

(beat)

MALCOLM. *(embarrassed)* I didn't, Wang, no.

DAVID. Yeah. Marco Polo must've been hitting that opium pipe a bit hard one night. Or else some creative concubine shaved herself a certain direction to emphasize her exotic charms, you know? Blow the stupid barbarian's mind?

MALCOLM. Huh. Well…that's weird. I never heard of that.

DAVID. Anyways. You had a good time?

MALCOLM. Amazing, yeah. It's funny, actually – not being able to speak? We got through a lot of bullshit early. No small talk. Straight to the point of stuff. Felt like we really…connected, in this weird way…

DAVID. Huh. That's good. Good. What about your little – problem area?

MALCOLM. Worked out.

DAVID. Apparently.

MALCOLM. I don't know how you knew, Wang, but – I have to say, it was some kind of sick genius –

DAVID. Knew what?

MALCOLM. Y'know – that we had the same – that she also has…?

(beat)

What?

DAVID. Nothing…

MALCOLM. No, tell me. What? Why are you –

DAVID. Xiao Mei doesn't have herpes, Malcolm.

MALCOLM. Yeah, she does, she…*(it dawns on him)* Wait, why? What are you – what'd you say to her, Wang? What'd you fucking say?

DAVID. I told her you have intimacy issues and don't know how to talk to people, so you're a little shy making first moves –

MALCOLM. What the fuck, man?!?

DAVID. It's true, right? And it worked out –

MALCOLM. No! No, it didn't – it didn't "work out," Wang. I was trying to be honest here! Do the right thing by –

DAVID. So? Tell her yourself. Once your Chinese gets better. She'll understand.

MALCOLM. It's a little bit late, now!

DAVID. Why? I thought you weren't supposed to be contagious.

MALCOLM. I'm not! Supposed to be, but –

DAVID. So? No harm done, right? You used precautions, didn't you?

MALCOLM. Of course, but –

DAVID. China's like – ground zero for efficient family planning, Malcolm. She knows the risks, believe me. Been hearing her whole life about the filthy corruptions of foreign invaders like you.

MALCOLM. That's not the point! It's called "informed consent"! She has a right to know what she's getting into with a new sexual partner when she –

DAVID. Don't quote me the Stanford Health Services brochure, Malcolm! Jesus Christ! All these years I've watched you – every girl you meet: "Hi, I'm Malcolm Ziegler and I have genital herpes. Type Two!" It's like you're spraying pussy repellent everywhere you go. Trying to keep people away from you. But now see? One time, you keep your big mouth shut, an actual *homo sapien* female likes you for a change. What a surprise! Maybe you're not so disgusting as you thought.

MALCOLM. I didn't "keep my mouth shut" though, Wang. I *asked* you to tell her something, and you – *lied* about it!

DAVID. So? You're seeing her tomorrow, right? Tell her yourself. Make it your first Chinese lesson. Blame it all on me. A translation mistake. Just wanted to give you a little dose of confidence, your first night in Beijing… figured you could probably use it.

(beat)

MALCOLM. You're a dick.

DAVID. Fine. I apologize for trying to get you ass. Now get dressed. I have to show you around the office today, so look presentable. Don't embarrass me in front of my countrymen.

*(**MALCOLM** looks at **DAVID**. He sighs.)*

MALCOLM. Unbelievable, man…am I allowed to shower this time at least?

DAVID. No time for that. Later. Why you want to wash that off anyway? Enjoy it while it lasts!

*(**MALCOLM** shakes his head, turns and digs through his duffel bag.)*

MALCOLM. What should I wear?

DAVID. Shirt and slacks is fine. We'll get you suits made this week. Today, I just take you around the office, introduce you to people. You don't have to talk. Just smile and say "nǐ hǎo" *[hello]*.

MALCOLM. What kind of office is it though? I don't think I even know what it is you do, Wang –

DAVID. Oh, little of this, little of that. I told you.

MALCOLM. Yeah, but I don't think I – you're some kind of…headhunter?

DAVID. Yeah, kind of.

*(**MALCOLM** starts getting dressed)*

I work with wài dì rén *[migrant workers]*, right? Who are looking for jobs –

MALCOLM. Foreigners.

DAVID. *(laughs)* No no…Bù shì. *[Not that.]* Foreigners is "Wài guó rén," Malcolm. "Outside country people." Wài dì rén just means – "people from outside," y'know. Migrant workers. Hicks from out of town.

MALCOLM. Okay…

DAVID. Millions of these poor nóngmín *[peasants]* come to Beijing every year to find work. We sign them up. At the train station, through friends, whatever. And then introduce them to companies that are hiring. People always need to find other people, right? We're like – Facebook for unemployed Chinese peasant labor.

MALCOLM. And how am I qualified to talk about –

DAVID. Just business, Malcolm. Like anything. Always good to have a smart guy around. Plus, everybody's very impressed to have a full-time lǎo wài *[foreigner]* around the office. Gives the company lots of face.

MALCOLM. So I'm – your white performing monkey?

DAVID. Until your Chinese gets better. You can keep your mouth shut and try to look American, right?

MALCOLM. I think I can handle that…

DAVID. Okay then.

MALCOLM. *(putting on a shirt)* Hey – can I you ask a question?

DAVID. Shoot.

MALCOLM. What's "xuě bì" mean?

DAVID. Sprite?

MALCOLM. No, but literally – the characters…?

DAVID. Oh. Xuě bì. "Snow Green."

MALCOLM. Uh-huh. That's – What about "shuǐ…bī"?

DAVID. Snowy cunt. Hey, you have some other shirt to wear, man? That's just – sad.

MALCOLM. Why, what's – *(giving up, switching shirts)* Doesn't that seem like – a bad choice for a brand name though? To be so close to –

DAVID. It's not close. Completely different tone. Like – "Coke" is not "cock" to you, right? Big difference.

Chinese would never make this mistake. Why? You offer Xiao Mei some wet pussy last night?

MALCOLM. Apparently…

DAVID. *(laughs)* Don't worry. Should have been other way around, I guess. But she'll forgive you.

MALCOLM. All right – how do I look?

(He's now dressed in slightly wrinkled shirts and slacks from his duffel.)

*(**DAVID** looks him over critically)*

DAVID. Very casual. Like you were sent over by a casting agency to play the typical part of the ignorant white guy…it's perfect.

SCENE 4

(A local dumpling restaurant)

(SAMANYA *and* **XIAO MEI** *open chopsticks, rub them together to remove any splinters, pour hot tea on their plates to get rid of germs.)*

SAMANYA. Tā shì zěnmeyàng de? *[So what's he like?]*

XIAO MEI. Who?

SAMANYA. Zhège – Měiguórén? *[This – American?]* Malcolm?

XIAO MEI. Nice.

SAMANYA. Wǒ men kěyǐ shuō Zhōngguó huà. *[We can speak Chinese.]*

XIAO MEI. No, I like – practice my English…it's okay?

SAMANYA. *(disappointed)* Yeah. Sure.

> *(beat)*

Seemed kinda gay to me.

XIAO MEI. No. Bù *[Not]* gay. I think – funny. Very – nervous?

SAMANYA. *(teasing)* Sexy.

XIAO MEI. Yes, kind of sexy. I think, he is out of his true place, nǐ tīng de dǒng ma? *[you know what I mean?]* Like me. Wǒ men hé de lái. *[We get along.]*

SAMANYA. Dave's quite the matchmaker, huh? Where'd he find you?

XIAO MEI. Sorry…"Find…?"

SAMANYA. I mean, how'd you two meet?

XIAO MEI. Oh, me and – Dà Wéi? From work.

SAMANYA. You work together? At his office?

XIAO MEI. No, I – teach. Chinese.

SAMANYA. And he needed lessons?

XIAO MEI. *(laughs)* No, but – the people he know need this sometime…

> *(beat)*

And you? How do you – meet Dà Wéi?

SAMANYA. *(embarrassed)* Oh, he picked me up at a club.

XIAO MEI. Zhēn de ma? *[Really?]*

SAMANYA. Yeah. Started chatting me up while I was dancing. Talking about the Olympics or some nonsense…and then right in the middle of a sentence, he put his hand up my skirt on my behind. I was like "What! This Zhōng guó xiǎo huǒzi *[Chinese guy]* has some serious nánzǐ hàn de fēngdù! *[machismo!]*

XIAO MEI. Wǒ de tiān! *[My God!]* *(laughs)* How do you say this in –

SAMANYA. "He's macho."

XIAO MEI. Yes…I think so too.

SAMANYA. Course, I was high off my ass on E at the time, so that could be a part of it…

XIAO MEI. "E"?

SAMANYA. Ecstacy? Um…yáo tóu wán. *[Shaking head pill.]*

XIAO MEI. "Shaking-the-head-pill."

(they both laugh)

SAMANYA. Cops raided the club that night. Busted in and let all the lǎo wài *[foreigners]* leave. And then made all the Chinese pee in a cup. Hauled 'em off to jail. Crazy, the double standard here, right? Tài bù gōng píng le. *[So unfair.]*

XIAO MEI. Mm…

SAMANYA. But Dave bribed one of the guards to let him out the back. Caught up with me in the alleyway outside. And I jumped his bones in the backseat of his Hummer.

XIAO MEI. Jumped his…?

SAMANYA. Wǒ men wánr le. *[We fucked.]*

XIAO MEI. Ah! Nàme suíbiàn! *[Very casual!]*

SAMANYA. Hey, we're modern girls, right?

XIAO MEI. Yes. True…

SAMANYA. So you? And Dave? Ever…?

XIAO MEI. Oh, no. Bù kě néng. *[Impossible.]*

SAMANYA. Never?

XIAO MEI. Cóng lái méiyǒu. *[Never.]*

SAMANYA. How come?

XIAO MEI. I think – maybe we are too different people?

SAMANYA. He likes different.

XIAO MEI. No, maybe different – in way he would not like. Money different?

SAMANYA. I don't think Dave cares about that...

> *(beat)*

> I don't.

XIAO MEI. Mm.

SAMANYA. I really don't.

XIAO MEI. *(nods)*

SAMANYA. I want to be friends...

XIAO MEI. Yes...me too.

SAMANYA. So...you plan to see this hairy lǎo wài *[foreigner]* again or what? We can double date.

> **(XIAO MEI** *smiles)*

XIAO MEI. Dāng rán. *[Of course.]* I am his Chinese tutor, yes?

SAMANYA. Ah...Pillow talk ma? *[huh?]*

> *(they laugh)*

SCENE 5

(**MALCOLM**'s *hotel room*)

(**MALCOLM** *and* **XIAO MEI** *sit on the bed, half-naked. Language workbooks and flashcards spread out on their laps.*)

(**MALCOLM** *reads from a piece of paper.*)

MALCOLM. Wǒ bìyè, zài wǒ de chē lǐ...*[After I graduate in my car...]*

XIAO MEI. Bù bù bù – *[No no no –]* (*corrects him*) Wǒ bì yè yǐ hòu. "After I graduate." Wǒ kāi chē "I drove my car." Not "After I graduate in my car."

MALCOLM. Duì. *[Yeah.]* Sorry. Um...wǒ kāi chē. *[I drove my car.]* How do you say – "alone"?

XIAO MEI. Wǒ jì mò le. *[I was lonely.]*

MALCOLM. Wǒ jì mò le. Shénme dōu méiyǒu...Dà Wéi ràng wǒ gōng zuò. Wǒ lái Beijing. Wǒ rènshi nǐ. Cóng nà yǐhòu yí bèi zi xìng fú shēng huó. *[I was lonely. Felt like I had nothing...Dà Wéi offered me a job. I came to Beijing. I met this girl. And lived happily ever after.]*

(*she claps*)

XIAO MEI. Very good, Mal-colm! After only three week improvement!

MALCOLM. Well...had a good teacher.

(*He kisses her. She pushes him away.*)

XIAO MEI. Stay to the lesson.

MALCOLM. Your turn.

XIAO MEI. No...

MALCOLM. Yes. Your turn. Come on.

(*she takes out a piece of paper, bites her lip*)

XIAO MEI. Uch...I don't know if this is correct way of saying thing, Mal-colm...many word I have to look up before I can –

MALCOLM. Here – I'll distract you.

(he kisses her neck)

(she laughs)

XIAO MEI. Mm. Very distracting…O-kay. So. *(clears her throat, reads:)* My name Wu Mei. Born in Henan Province… single child…mother and father these traditional farming folk. Have no money. No son to help the work. But mother – she have some modern idea in her head. Do not want this life for me, like she have had. Want to help me táo zǒu *[escape]* from this.

MALCOLM. *(kissing down her shoulder)* Hm.

XIAO MEI. So – when I turn to sixteen, she allow me begin to date the young mens. Not proper Chinese daughter for my bà ba *[dad]* in this way, but…one of these mens, he want to keep me. Fall in love and proposition for me…

MALCOLM. Proposed.

XIAO MEI. Mm. He proposed for me. Xiè xie nǐ *[Thank you]*, Mal-colm. We are having beer at festival in Luoyang, and he ask "Marry to me, Mei Mei." And I am very drunk at this time…I shout "Oh ha ha! What are you talking, melon head?" And I fall over into sleep. "Pass out," duì ma? *[right?]*

MALCOLM. You got it. Good use.

XIAO MEI. Then. Next day, he is very embarrass. Ashame. Want to forget this diūmiànzi de sh. *[loss of face.]* Tell the town-folk he have to leave me now, for I am this wanton woman.

MALCOLM. *(laughs)* "Wanton"?

XIAO MEI. Not right?

MALCOLM. Uh. It's a little old-fashioned, but –

XIAO MEI. What word?

MALCOLM. I don't know. "Easy"? Maybe.

XIAO MEI. "Easy"? He tell people I am this easy woman…?

MALCOLM. Mm-hm.

XIAO MEI. O-kay. Not true I am this easy, Mal-colm, understand? I think, actually, I am more harder at this time, than now…but this talk for people mean I have to leave my bà ba's *[father's]* home. Do not say when I will go, just – take bus to Beijing without goodbye.

(he takes off her skirt)

XIAO MEI. Mal-colm…

MALCOLM. Come on. Keep going. It's good.

(he touches her while she reads, kisses her back)

(reads) So. In Beijing, I find new work…make new life and see many new thing. "Start over," duì ma? *[yes?]* One time, see some foreigner at discotheque. Casual folk, laughing, singing, shouting together…and I think, I am like this now. A foreigner. In my new life. Free and live only for myself. "Selfish," shì bù shì? *[right?]*

MALCOLM. No.

XIAO MEI. What word?

MALCOLM. No, I mean – I don't think it's selfish, Mei. That you get to live your own life. The way you want. Self-sufficient, maybe.

XIAO MEI. Suff-ish-ent.

MALCOLM. Like – you can take care of yourself?

XIAO MEI. Ah. Very American idea, duì ma? *[isn't it?]*

MALCOLM. You think so?

XIAO MEI. Yes, rich folk idea.

MALCOLM. Ha. Well, maybe, yeah. Never thought of it like that…

(beat)

Oh hey, speaking of which –

(he reaches for his money belt)

MALCOLM. I still owe you, you know, for all the –

XIAO MEI. Oh, no. No –

MALCOLM. We haven't ever –

XIAO MEI. Dà Wéi arrange for lesson, Mal-colm –

MALCOLM. Yeah, but – only twice a week, right? And you've been here almost every night for like –

XIAO MEI. I think for English is fair trade.

MALCOLM. Yeah, but. Three weeks of work. Let me at least give you a –

(she stops him)

XIAO MEI. Bù hǎo yìsi *[I'm embarrassed]*. No money, okay? Bù hé shì *[Not appropriate]*. In this romantic situation…

(beat)

MALCOLM. Okay, yeah…you're right. *(he puts the money away)* You know we don't have to stay in the hotel though, right? I could take you out, at least, sometimes, if you –

XIAO MEI. Why not in? We have bed here. Book. Xuě bì. *[Sprite.]*

MALCOLM. *(laughs)*

XIAO MEI. Everything we need, shì bù shì? *[right?]*

MALCOLM. Dāng rán. *[Of course.]* But maybe we could go to your place. Sometime…I'd love to meet your friends, you know? See where you live, and –

XIAO MEI. Not fancy place.

MALCOLM. I don't care about that. It doesn't matter. What it looks like. I just want to know where you're from, is all.

XIAO MEI. Maybe some time…

MALCOLM. And I understand, you know. What you're talking about…I mean I was always – alienated from people too. In New Jersey? Know what I mean by that? Alienated?

(she doesn't)

I had a lot of trouble. Relating, is what I – I dropped out. Just left, like you. Without saying anything to anyone…I wanted to táo zǒu *[escape]* my life too.

XIAO MEI. Wèi shénme? *[Why?]* If you are so – free there?

MALCOLM. Oh, because. Y'know, maybe – I didn't feel free? Or maybe because I knew there was something else out there for me. Better than being free...you.

XIAO MEI. *(laughs)* So cheesy, Mal-colm! Tài ròumá le! *[Gives me the shivers!]*

MALCOLM. Anyway, very nice essay.

(they kiss, and she wraps her legs around him)

MALCOLM. And hey, Xiao Mei?

XIAO MEI. Mm?

MALCOLM. Can I ask you something else? Something – important?

XIAO MEI. Impotent?

MALCOLM. Important.

XIAO MEI. *(she's teasing him)* Impotent.

MALCOLM. *(laughs)* Yeah, I'm – still on a sixty day visa here, you know? A tourist visa. So I have to leave China, for a bit, before I can come back in?

XIAO MEI. Shénme shíhou? *[When?]*

MALCOLM. Like two weeks from now? But I was thinking, y'know...maybe – You could come with me? When I go?

(beat)

XIAO MEI. Wǒ bù dǒng. *[I don't understand.]*

MALCOLM. Like on a trip. We could travel together? To the States or – see some sights? I don't know. Take a vacation. What do you think?

XIAO MEI. I think, Mal-colm, American visa only for student...rich dàwàn er *[big shots]* and government official.

MALCOLM. Yeah, but you have a passport, don't you?

XIAO MEI. Of course, but no – foreign paper for this type travel.

MALCOLM. Well, let me see what I can do. Use my "guānxi" *[connections]* right? Couldn't hurt to try.

XIAO MEI. You would ask Dà Wéi this favor.

MALCOLM. Wang, yeah.

XIAO MEI. He will not want to do this for us, Mal-colm.

MALCOLM. Of course he would, he –

XIAO MEI. No. Maybe…some part of Dà Wéi you cannot understand so much, but –

MALCOLM. Come on. I'm sure he'd love to. Arrange some paperwork for his friends? He does it all the time, for perfect strangers, right?

XIAO MEI. Yes, but – His nóng nú *[indentured servants]*, you mean? For make money, Mal-colm. Not for friendship.

MALCOLM. "Nóng nú"? What's – (MALCOLM *flips through the dictionary*)

XIAO MEI. Don't know if English word for –

MALCOLM. Slaves?

XIAO MEI. No. Bù shì *[not]* "slaves." His – worker with debt. On the farm, or…? Anyway, not really for me to talk about Dà Wéi like this with you. I hope you would not tell him I –

MALCOLM. No, of course. Don't worry.

XIAO MEI. Cannot ask him. For this visa, Mal-colm. O-kay? He would kěn dìng *[definitely]* not understand.

MALCOLM. All right. Just between us, huh? And hey – fuck Wang. All right? This has nothing to do with him. It's our own guānxi. *[relationship.]* I'm saying *I* want you to come to New York. Visit the States. With me. I think without seeing my country you bù kě néng *[impossible]* can understand me for real, nǐ zhīdào *[you understand]?*

XIAO MEI. Mm.

MALCOLM. Gimme your passport. All right? I'll take care of everything.

XIAO MEI. But Mal-colm –

MALCOLM. For me. Not for you. It's something I want. *Selfishly.* Because I'm falling in love with you…

(*she smiles*)

XIAO MEI. Xíng. *[Okay.]* If you think this is good idea,

Mal-colm...Wǒ xiāng xìn nǐ. *[I will trust you.]*

MALCOLM. Yeah, trust me. Do. This is gonna be a lot of fun...

SCENE 6

(**DAVID**'s *office*)

(*The room is sleek, modern, with a few traditional Chinese touches – wood lattice screens, expensive paper scrolls, a bronze toad on the desk.*)

(*Mirrored plate glass windows overlook a sprawl of construction outside.*)

(**DAVID** *stands by the window, talking on a bluetooth earpiece.*)

DAVID. Lǎo Chen, Lǎo Chen – wǒ míng bái nǐde yì sī – ràng wǒ shuō huà ba...nà nǐ wèishéme gěi wǒ dǎ diàn huà? Bù. Bù, wǒ men bǎi fēn zhī yī bǎi de – [*Old Chen, Old Chen – I realize what you're saying, just – if you'd give me a minute to talk...well then, what are you calling me about it for? No. No, we absolutely one hundred percent –]*

(*a knock on the door*)

DAVID. Jìn lái ba, uh. [*Come in.*]

(**MALCOLM** *enters, wearing a new tailored suit.*)

(**DAVID** *switches rapidly between English and Chinese:*)

Have a seat, Malc. Be just a sec here, I – (*into the phone*) Nǐ yīng gāi zhíjiē lái zhǎo wǒ, bù yīng gāi zì jǐ gàn – [*You're supposed to come to me directly, not handle it all by your –]*

(*to* **MALCOLM**) Big client. Massive fucking stone in my – (*into the phone*) Méiyǒu, wǒ zài gēn wǒ de mì shū jiǎng huà-ne Chen xiān sheng, shuō yīng yǔ. Qǐng nín jì xù. [*No, I'm speaking to my secretary, Mister Chen. In English. Please, continue.*]

(*to* **MALCOLM**) How're things?

MALCOLM. Good. Good, should I –

DAVID. No no, it's fine – Sit. Relax.

(**MALCOLM** *looks for a place to sit, remains standing*)

DAVID. *(into the phone)* Dàn shì wǒ men kàn bù jiàn wǒ men gōng rén de xīn lǐ xiǎng de shì shěn-me, Chen xiān sheng. Wǒ zěnme zhī dào tā shì gè huì dǎo luàn de rén, wǒ gēn běn – *[But we can't see into the thoughts of all our employees, Mister Chen. How was I supposed to know he was a troublemaker when I –]*

(to **MALCOLM***)* Prick runs a metals plant in Guang Dong. Recycled aluminum and nickel? Total shit-kicker, but –

(into the phone) Dāng rán. Dāng rán...wǒ huì chǔ lǐ zhège dǎoluàn fèn zi. *[Of course. Of course...I'll deal with the trouble maker myself.]*

(to **MALCOLM***)* Worked his way up from collecting tin cans on his bicycle cart. Started a factory. Cornered the local market. Now he's a big ass dàwàn er *[big shot]* – Owns fifty cars, molests all the little girls on his assembly line, and thinks he's fucking Andrew Carnegie...

(into the phone) Nín yǒu měi yǒu shōu dào wǒ jì gěi nín de xuě jiā? *[Did you get the cigars I sent?]*

(to **MALCOLM***)* Only he can't read and washes his nuts once in a blue –

(into the phone) Hǎo hǎo hǎo. Gēn nín shuō huà yǒng yuǎn shì gè róng xìng, Lǎo Chen. Nín shì wǒ zuì xǐ huān de kè hù le. Zài liánxì, uh? *[Good, good...Always a pleasure to chat with you, Lao Chen. You're my favorite client. Talk to you later, okay?]* Fucking peasant. I hope you get executed.

(he disconnects the call)

MALCOLM. Ha. What's that about?

DAVID. Ach, nothing, man. Labor dispute he's dealing with...one of our guys maybe the ring leader. Blah blah blah –

MALCOLM. So what do we do?

DAVID. Do? We take care of it.

MALCOLM. How?

DAVID. *(shrugs)* China's not about to let a bunch of ragtag farmhands get in the way of ten point three percent annual GDP growth. Mister Chen's aluminum is used to make cars and cans and watches and wires and industrial supplies – all vital international exports.

MALCOLM. So what? They'll be arrested?

DAVID. Nah, they'll just be – discouraged from further anti-social activities. For the good of the People…*(smiles)* You grew up in the richest country on Earth, Malcolm. So I know you don't have to think about this stuff too much…but come on. How do you think it got to be that way? Sweatshops, right? Migrant workers. Coolies. Slaves. They built up your country so now everyone can afford to be free there. But China's in the midst of her own industrial revolution now. You can't apply contemporary American standards here…

(beat)

Anyway, tell me something more interesting, man! Take my mind off boring work! How's the office treating you?

MALCOLM. It's – ridiculous, Wang. I sit at my desk in that enormous glass fishbowl all day and – make paper airplanes. Play solitaire. We've got – Senior VP's with offices half the size of mine. It's embarrassing. I'm sure they all resent the hell out of me.

DAVID. Yeah, they do…hey, what are you up to the first day of Chinese New Year?

MALCOLM. I'm – supposed to go out with Xiao Mei, I think.

DAVID. Oh, where to?

MALCOLM. Houhai Lake?

DAVID. Houhai. Supposed to be the most romantic place in all Beijing. Of course, it smells like raw sewage, but Chinese apparently don't notice this at all, or –

MALCOLM. "Chinese"?

DAVID. *(grins)* Four years in Palo Alto ruined my nose! All of Asia smells like a giant toilet bowl to me now.

MALCOLM. I like it better. Feels more – alive here. I never realized it was so antiseptic, back home.

DAVID. "Clean," you mean?

MALCOLM. Sterile.

DAVID. First world? *(putting his feet on his desk)* So what can I do for you then? Just drop by to chat?

MALCOLM. No. No, I wanted to – ask a favor, Wang, actually. If you're not too –

DAVID. Oh yeah? Shoot.

MALCOLM. Feel like an ingrate, with everything you've already – I mean, I don't know what you get out of all this, honestly. Given what a horrendous employee I've been, but –

DAVID. Get to repay my debts, man…

MALCOLM. What debts?

DAVID. Freshman year. You know…

(off **MALCOLM**'s *blank look)*

Come on, Malcolm. You remember. My first day? Freshman orientation? Walk into that dorm feeling like Charlie Chan? With my funny name. Bad teeth. Broken-ass English. *(laughs)* I never felt alone like that in my life! Sitting by myself, thinking I should run back to China, tail between my legs…and then this skinny kid comes up to me, in a Star Wars t-shirt – takes me around campus. Sits by me in the dining hall. I was trying not to cry that whole first week, man, swear to God…so grateful to you for being there. And you were always happy to hang out too. Never seem to mind my cramping your style –

MALCOLM. *(trying to joke)* What style?

DAVID. You were white, man. Style enough, over there…

MALCOLM. Well, I think we can consider the Freshman year obligations seriously paid at this point, Wang, all right? You've been more generous to me since then than I could ever –

DAVID. Not about being generous, Malcolm. I lost a lot of face, being the ignorant foreigner over there. I'm trying to return the favor –

MALCOLM. And you have! Believe me, I just –

DAVID. So spit it out. Bù yào kè qi. *[Don't be polite.]* Anything for my lǎo péngyou *[old friend]*, right? Something wrong with the hotel?

MALCOLM. The hotel? Yeah, it's too fancy. I miss sleeping with a gearshift up my ass.

DAVID. *(laughs)* What then?

MALCOLM. I was – just between us, I was hoping you could work out a little visa issue for me, Wang…

DAVID. Oh yeah?

MALCOLM. Yeah. You know my sixty days are half up here? I have to take a trip, out of the country, this month, before I can –

DAVID. Yeah, I was thinking – we'll go to Macao together, all right? It's like – this Chinese version of Las Vegas? But way bigger? And better. Fucking crazier, like everything else here…whole island of baccarat, Cantonese whores, and all-you-can-eat 24-hour dim sum.

MALCOLM. Sounds – amazing, Wang, I –

DAVID. I'll hook it up.

MALCOLM. Well, but – I was actually – I was thinking of… maybe this time – inviting Xiao Mei to visit the States with me. If you think that's –

DAVID. Oh, no shit…she put you up to this?

MALCOLM. No. No, I just –

DAVID. I thought you hated life in the States, Malcolm…

MALCOLM. I think – I'd like it better with her there.

DAVID. Really? How long we talking?

MALCOLM. I don't know.

DAVID. A week? Two weeks?

MALCOLM. As long as she wants, I guess…I mean – if that's something you can work out…on such short notice, or –

DAVID. Sure, I can. I *can*, yeah. Why? You two getting serious on me?

MALCOLM. I just thought – it'd be nice, you know?

DAVID. It would be nice.

MALCOLM. To thank her – for everything she's done for me, and –

DAVID. *(laughs)* Same old Malcolm, man…

MALCOLM. What?

DAVID. This droopy liberal guilt trip…you act like you just deflowered Mulan here! But it's the 21st Century in China. Nobody expects you to light yourself on fire over a one-night stand!

MALCOLM. I'm not, I just – I think she'd like to see the world…

DAVID. Of course she would.

MALCOLM. And you know she'd never met anyone from outside her village before she came to Beijing, Wang? People there couldn't even read. Now she's teaching Chinese to foreigners. Reading *Harry Potter*. Listening to Erasure –

DAVID. Pulled herself up by her bootstraps.

MALCOLM. In a way –

DAVID. The American Dream.

MALCOLM. Well, but in America, this kind of thing never happens anymore, right? It's just like – some bullshit myth from a long time ago. But here it's for real. Today. She's created this whole new identity, out of thin air. Reminds me of like – Gatsby or something.

DAVID. Except with long hair and a sideways vagina.

(beat)

I'm sorry, just – what do you know about this girl, man? Really.

MALCOLM. I know – what I need to know.

DAVID. Which is what? Exactly? Lot of foreigners come here, remember, want to take home an exotic souvenir…a pearl from the Orient. I'm just telling you – it's the oldest story in all of China.

MALCOLM. But this isn't – "exotic," Wang. At all. If anything, it's the opposite of – she makes me feel more – familiar. Can you understand that? More comfortable in my own skin. I can be more myself, when I'm around her, and –

DAVID. You can see inside each other.

MALCOLM. In a way...

DAVID. Tell each other everything.

MALCOLM. I guess so.

DAVID. You tell her about the herpes yet?

(beat)

Come on, man. Get laid. Have fun. That's what tourists do. But don't run off with the first mysterious xiǎo jiē *[lady]* who lets you look at her bí. *[cunt.]* Trust me. I'm looking out for you here...

(beat)

MALCOLM. Yeah. You're right.

DAVID. Yeah?

MALCOLM. Yeah, sorry to bother you with this, Wang...I know you're super busy. Maybe we could keep this to ourselves though, huh? *(opens the door)* Suàn lē bā *[Never mind]*, okay? It was just a thought...

SCENE 7

(Houhai Lake)

(**MALCOLM** *and* **XIAO MEI**, *under the trees on a concrete bench.*)

(It sounds like a street fair outside: cart vendors, people laughing, a busker playing an erhu.*)*

(**XIAO MEI** *nibbles a fried calamari skewer on a stick.*)

XIAO MEI. Yān huǒ mǎ shàng jiù yào kāi shǐ. *[Fireworks are about to start.]*

MALCOLM. Yān huǒ?

XIAO MEI. Fire-work.

MALCOLM. Oh, when?

XIAO MEI. Soon.

MALCOLM. Cool…I love fireworks.

XIAO MEI. Of course. Měiguó rén. *[Americans.]* Love all thing "Made in China."

MALCOLM. *(laughs)* Yeah, I guess that's true…

(they watch the sky)

MALCOLM. So – Mei. You have any resolutions to make?

XIAO MEI. Hm?

MALCOLM. Resolutions…? In the States, on the New Year, we make like – little promises to ourselves? To be better people, or –

XIAO MEI. Kěn dìng *[Definitely]*. I promise.

MALCOLM. No, I mean specific, like – people might promise to lose some weight or –

XIAO MEI. It's a good idea. Because many Chinese are now also becoming fat like Americans.

MALCOLM. Yeah, but – *(laughs)* No, I mean it could be anything. You could just – promise to be nicer to people. Or work harder at something? Learn ballroom dancing. Visit your in-laws. It's just – a chance to change something. About yourself, that you think you should –

XIAO MEI. Promise to better my English?

(beat)

MALCOLM. Yeah. Okay. Good…

XIAO MEI. You?

MALCOLM. Mine is to be more – open about myself, I think…

XIAO MEI. *(teasing)* Already too open, Mal-colm. Need to promise more close.

MALCOLM. Well, but there's something I've been meaning to…get off my chest, Xiao Mei. Something that's been bothering me, for a while now. I don't want to have any secrets between us, and –

XIAO MEI. Wèi shénme? *[What?]*

MALCOLM. I have – kind of a confession to make…

XIAO MEI. Con-fesh-un?

MALCOLM. Tǎn bái. *[Confession.]*

XIAO MEI. Mal-colm, bù xū yào – *[not necessary –]*

MALCOLM. I want to. I want to. It's important, to me, y'know, that we're able to tell each other about ourselves, without –

XIAO MEI. Shénme yìsi? *[Why?]*

MALCOLM. Because. I want to know you. Understand? Everything about you. Who you are. Where you've been. And I want you to know the same about me, because –

XIAO MEI. You know this about me already, Mal-colm.

MALCOLM. I don't though. Not really…

XIAO MEI. Best part of knowing –

MALCOLM. But I don't want the best part. I want all of it. Everything –

XIAO MEI. Ask.

(Beat. He smiles.)

MALCOLM. I don't know the right questions...

(the sound of distant fireworks exploding over the lake)

(the light is reflected on their faces)

MALCOLM. You ever been in love?

XIAO MEI. Yes.

MALCOLM. How many times?

XIAO MEI. Two.

MALCOLM. Am I one of them?

XIAO MEI. *(laughs)* Mal-colm...You know this already.

MALCOLM. But you've never said it –

XIAO MEI. Don't have to say this in words...

MALCOLM. Who's the other one?

XIAO MEI. His name Paul.

MALCOLM. American?

XIAO MEI. From Canada.

(beat)

MALCOLM. So what happened?

XIAO MEI. We are not right for each other, in the end...

MALCOLM. But what about –

(XIAO MEI *takes* **MALCOLM***'s face and kisses him, shutting him up for a moment.)*

(when he pulls away, she holds him there, looks into his eyes)

XIAO MEI. Wǒ men de *[our]* resolution, Mal-colm. Can be – to trust this here. *This.* Without con-fesh-un in words. Hǎo bù hǎo? *[good or not good?]*

(he looks at her)

MALCOLM. Hǎo. *[Good.]*

XIAO MEI. O-kay?

MALCOLM. Yeah. You're right, Mei...thanks. For bringing me out here. I really –

XIAO MEI. Méi wèn tí *[No problem].* I am glad. To show you some of my Beijing…*(quoting him:)* "Without this, you bù kě néng *[impossible]* can understand me for real, shì bù shì? *[right?]*"

*(**MALCOLM** smiles, recognizing his own words)*

MALCOLM. Yeah. That's true…And look – *(He takes out a printout of an e-ticket.)* Check it out. I got the tickets. See? Beijing to JFK. We leave in a week, if you're still –

XIAO MEI. Mal-colm – Nà wǒde visa ne? *[And my visa?]*

MALCOLM. I'm taking care of it.

XIAO MEI. You will not ask Dà Wéi for this –

MALCOLM. I got other tricks up my sleeve. Okay? Let me worry about that. You just tell me what you want to see…

XIAO MEI. Your home-town?

MALCOLM. Ha. Hoboken? You can do better…we're flying into New York. So we can visit Chinatown, if you feel homesick –

XIAO MEI. *(wrinkles her nose)* Cantonese folk in America Chinatown, Mal-colm. Eat anything with four legs, including table.

MALCOLM. Okay, fine. So we'll eat Western food, huh? Hamburgers and ketchup, the entire time. Whatever you like. And hey – listen. If you want, Mei, we could always stay in the States longer. You know? For more than a week? If you felt like it.

XIAO MEI. Nǐ shénmeyìsi? *[What do you mean?]*

MALCOLM. *(a kind of proposal)* I just mean…if I go home, I want you to come with me. I want us to be together. Wherever we are.

XIAO MEI. Wǒ yě shì. *[Me too.]*

MALCOLM. Yeah?

XIAO MEI. Dāng rán *[Of course]*, Mal-colm. Even in Ho-bo-ken…

MALCOLM. Ha. Well. All right then…

(They sit there for a moment, watching the fireworks.)

(she puts her head on his shoulder, nibbles her squid)

(he watches her)

SCENE 8

(An ex-pat cafe)

(**MALCOLM** *and* **SAMANYA** *at a table, drinking iced tea*)

MALCOLM. So thanks…for meeting up with me on such short –

SAMANYA. Oh, please. Any friend of Dave's, right? And Mei's…Gōng xǐ nǐ *[Congratulations]*, man. She's a catch. Hope it all works out for you guys…

MALCOLM. Yeah, me too, that's actually – I wanted to ask a favor, Samanya. If you don't mind my –

SAMANYA. Go ahead. Bù yào kè qi *[Don't be polite.]*

MALCOLM. Your dad…Mei says he's a diplomat?

SAMANYA. Last I checked.

MALCOLM. Yeah, so I was just wondering…I mean I know we don't know each other that well. Yet. But you know, I'm trying to get her a visa to come to the States with me?

SAMANYA. Oh yeah?

MALCOLM. Yeah. And I thought – you might be able to help with –

SAMANYA. He works at the *Cameroonian* embassy, Malcolm. You want to visit Yaoundé?

MALCOLM. *(laughs)* No, but I thought…he must know people, right? Have some guānxi *[connections]*? With other embassies…?

SAMANYA. Why not ask Dave?

MALCOLM. She doesn't want me to.

SAMANYA. How come?

MALCOLM. Oh, I guess…she thinks – he wouldn't approve?

SAMANYA. She didn't say why?

MALCOLM. Sometimes hard to tell with her. Maybe she just doesn't want the obligation? Or she feels embarrassed to ask? You know how shy she is, and –

SAMANYA. *(laughs)* Mei?

MALCOLM. What?

SAMANYA. I don't really think of her as "shy," Malcolm. Maybe about her English, but…*(teasing him)* That night you met. Shy or bù *[not]* shy?

MALCOLM. *(laughs)* No, but – there's just a lot of things we can't say to each other, you know.

SAMANYA. *(teasing, in French) Entre deux coeurs qui s'aiment, nul besoin de paroles…*

MALCOLM. Um…?

SAMANYA. "Two hearts in love need no words…"

MALCOLM. Ha. Yeah. Jesus. How many languages do you speak anyway?

SAMANYA. Oh, four and a half, I guess…

MALCOLM. Wow.

SAMANYA. For all the good it does me…use my French at embassy cocktail parties. Arabic to order fancy drinks at Uigher nightclubs. Chinese to take taxis to different shopping malls. And Bantu to argue with my mom about why I can't find a husband. I can say "I'm a grown woman! Let me lead my own life you bitch!" in perfect Ngumba dialect. But it's not like I'm working at the U.N., negotiating peace treaties or anything. Trust me.

MALCOLM. At least you could be. Negotiating. If I showed up at the U.N., they'd put me to work cleaning the toilets right away…

SAMANYA. But you're American, right, Malcolm? Fuck the U.N.! You own those toilets!

MALCOLM. *(laughs)* It's a relief, you know. To talk to another foreigner…kind of forgot what it feels like…

SAMANYA. Why not talk to Dave?

MALCOLM. Oh, he feels kind of – more Chinese to me, honestly, the longer I stay here…

SAMANYA. Hm.

MALCOLM. And even Mei – there's certain things...I try to understand, and it's like –

SAMANYA. Her English –

MALCOLM. No. No, it's – more than that. It's like...

(beat)

You know, we were over at Houhai the other night? Talking. And she was eating this – this squid on a stick, you know?

SAMANYA. Yóu yú chuàn. *[Calamari skewer.]*

MALCOLM. Yeah, this kind of – grilled sea monster? With the tentacles and everything? We were having this conversation, and suddenly I was like – oh my God. You know? Who is this woman? Where am I? What the hell am I doing here? Honestly. I was terrified.

SAMANYA. *(laughs)* Because of the squid? They're good!

MALCOLM. Yeah, I know. It's ridiculous. I just – I suddenly realized – her whole life, Mei's been eating nothing but Chinese food! Isn't that – weird?

SAMANYA. Not really, Malcolm...she's Chinese.

MALCOLM. Yeah, but I mean – her body isn't made of – bacon and eggs and Cheerios. All the stuff I'm used to...it's made of like – dofu and beansprouts! Yóu yú chuàn *[calamari skewer]*. How insane is that? We're literally made up of different materials...

SAMANYA. *(sympathetic)* Culture shock'll fuck you up. It'll pass.

MALCOLM. But at the same time, when I look at her? I swear, we recognize each other. Deep down...I know Wang thinks it's bullshit, but underneath all that – language, culture, food. There's something else.

(beat)

SAMANYA. Tell you what, Malcolm...I'd like to help. If I can. Why don't you get me her passport sometime, all right? And I'll –

(**MALCOLM** *slides* **XIAO MEI**'s *passport across the table,
a bit too quickly – he already had it out and ready.*)

(*they both smile*)

SAMANYA. I'll see what I can do...

SCENE 9

(**DAVID**'s house. A remodeled siheyaun [courtyard house] in a Beijing hutong [traditional alley neighborhood].)

(**SAMANYA** sits on the emperor bed, waiting, while **DAVID** changes clothes in his walk-in closet.)

DAVID. So what'd you tell him?

SAMANYA. I said sure. No big deal, right? Between friends. I sent it to the hotel this morning.

DAVID. Uh-huh. And when do they leave?

SAMANYA. Sunday. He already had the tickets. Just needed the paperwork taken care of...hey, you coming or what? I wanna go dancing!

(**DAVID** finally comes out, dressed to go clubbing.)

SAMANYA. I have never seen a man care so much about his clothes...

DAVID. You didn't feel the need to ask me about this?

SAMANYA. Why? I couldn't think of any reason you'd say no...

DAVID. Well, that's why you ask, right?

(beat)

SAMANYA. What's going on with you two?

DAVID. Nothing. He's just being a little bitch about work – having a hard time in China...

SAMANYA. I meant her.

DAVID. I think they're making a mistake, that's all.

SAMANYA. How come?

DAVID. They're not right for each other...

SAMANYA. How do you know?

DAVID. I know them.

SAMANYA. He wants her to see where he's from...it's romantic.

DAVID. For him maybe.

SAMANYA. Not like you've ever been to Cameroon...

DAVID. What do you want me to say? It's not a good match. I'm not gonna lie about it.

SAMANYA. They're in love.

DAVID. They only *think* they're in love.

SAMANYA. But you know better.

DAVID. I do, in this case, actually, yeah...

SAMANYA. And why is that?

DAVID. They're very different people.

SAMANYA. How so?

DAVID. Their education. Their backgrounds. Come on – the entire context of their lives...their future expectations. I mean what are they gonna do? Go back to her village in Henan? Meet her whole nóngmín *[peasant]* family? Live in a mud fucking hut the rest of their lives, farming beancurd? Of course not!

SAMANYA. How is it any of your business?

DAVID. I'm looking out for my friend.

SAMANYA. He's a big boy.

DAVID. He's a child. It would take Malcolm ten thousand fucking years to grasp the most basic assumptions that underlie her world view. All right? They're complete *strangers* to each other! So whatever *connection* they think they made here –

SAMANYA. You're an asshole.

DAVID. Come on – don't pretend to be offended by this. You know exactly what I'm talking about...

SAMANYA. I do, yeah. He's lǎo wài. *[a foreigner.]* And she's Chinese.

DAVID. No, he's a college kid from Stanford and she's a wài dì *[peasant]* shit farmer from some dump near Luoyang!

SAMANYA. So?

DAVID. So it's a bridge too far.

SAMANYA. *(re: the space between them)* And what about this?

DAVID. You're overreacting.

SAMANYA. Am I? How would you know? Maybe this is how Africans are supposed to react.

DAVID. This isn't about you.

SAMANYA. I didn't say it's about me. I think it's about you. And her.

DAVID. Her?

SAMANYA. I think you have a thing for this girl, Dave.

DAVID. *(scoffs)* You obviously don't know me very well.

SAMANYA. Better than you know yourself, sometimes…

DAVID. I don't date Chinese girls, remember?

SAMANYA. No, you date foreigners.

DAVID. And? Something wrong with that?

SAMANYA. Not if it's about me. Or any one single person. But if it starts to feel like a general foreigner fetish, I'd say it suggests a certain kind of self-loathing…

DAVID. And what about you?

SAMANYA. What about me what?

DAVID. You date foreigners too.

SAMANYA. I date Chinese guys. I come from China.

(**DAVID** *laughs in her face*)

(*beat*)

(*she gathers her purse*)

You know, I don't actually feel like dancing tonight…

DAVID. Fine. You want to go to Cameroon? We'll go.

SAMANYA. I don't want to go to Cameroon.

DAVID. What then?

SAMANYA. I want to stay here!

DAVID. So stay!

SAMANYA. I've never even met your parents…you know that? And they live six blocks from here.

DAVID. You wouldn't like them.

SAMANYA. They wouldn't like me, you mean…

DAVID. What's the difference? You wouldn't like each other. We've been over this.

SAMANYA. *(going to the door)* It's funny, you know…my whole life, I've always told people, "Yeah, China's racist. Suspicious of outsiders. Won't let you become a citizen, even if you were born here…but if you speak the language. Learn the culture. If you fall in love with a Chinese guy, have some half-Chinese babies…who's to say you don't belong?" Right?

(she opens the door)

See you, Wang Dà Wéi. It was nice knowing you…

SCENE 10

(**XIAO MEI**'s *apartment. A small, neat room in a suite she shares with three other women.*)

(**XIAO MEI** *is alone, packing her roller bag.*)

(*a knock on the door*)

XIAO MEI. Shéi? *[Who is it?]*

(*the door opens and* **DAVID** *enters*)

DAVID. Nǐ hǎo, Xiǎo Jiě. *[Hello, Miss.]*

XIAO MEI. (*surprised*) Dà Wéi...Nǐ lái gàn ma? *[What are you doing here?]*

(**DAVID** *looks around* **XIAO MEI**'s *apartment*)

DAVID. Bú cuò...*[Nice place...]*

XIAO MEI. Bù yào nàme kè qi. Nǐ yào shénme? *[I don't need polite talk. What do you want?]*

DAVID. Yào gēn nǐ tán yī tán. *[Just want to talk.]*

XIAO MEI. Tán shěnme? *[Talk about what?]*

DAVID. Kè jiāo de zěnme yàng? *[How are the lessons going?]*

XIAO MEI. Hěn hǎo. Tā yǒu le jìn bù...*[Good. He's coming along...]*

DAVID. (*re: the suitcase*) Qù lǚyóu ma? *[Going on a little trip, huh?]*

XIAO MEI. Duì. *[Yeah.]*

DAVID. Nǐ yào biànchéng Měiguórén ma? *[You want to become American now?]*

XIAO MEI. Shì tā de zhǔ yì, Dà Wéi. Bù shì wǒ de. *[It was his idea, Dà Wéi. Not mine.]*

DAVID. Shì zhèyàng ma? *[Is that right?]*

(**DAVID** *walks around, casually examining* **XIAO MEI**'s *belongings.*)

Nǐ shì zěnme ná dào qiān zhèng de? *[So how'd you get your visa?]*

XIAO MEI. Shì tā bāng wǒ bàn de. *[He got it.]*

DAVID. Wèi shénme méi ràng wǒ bāng nǐ bàn? *[Why didn't you come to me?]*

XIAO MEI. Yīnwéi wǒ zhīdào nǐ bù huì yuàn yì de. *[I knew you'd say no.]*

DAVID. Wèi shénme? Yīnwèi wǒ nà me xiàng Měiguórén, ma? *[And why is that? Because I'm so American?]*

XIAO MEI. Bù shì, yīnwéi nǐ shì Zhōngguórén…gēn wǒ yīyàng. *[No, because you're so Chinese…like me.]*

DAVID. Gēn nǐ yīyàng, ma? *[Like you, huh?]*

(he laughs, takes a glass bottle of erguotou from his jacket pocket, takes a swig directly from the bottle, sucks his teeth)

Ach…

XIAO MEI. Nǐ hē duōle… *[You're drunk…]*

DAVID. Méiyǒu. Wǒ wèi nǐ qìng zhù. *[No. We're celebrating.]*

(He offers her the bottle. She refuses.)

XIAO MEI. Nǐ yào shénme? *[What do you want?]*

(He walks over to her, takes her face in one hand, and kisses her roughly on the mouth.)

(she pulls away)

Bié zhèyàng – *[Don't do that –]*

DAVID. Wèi shénme bù? *[Why not?]*

XIAO MEI. Wǒ àishàng Mal-colm le. *[I'm in love with MALCOLM.]*

DAVID. Bù kě néng. *[Not possible.]*

XIAO MEI. Wèi shénma bù kě néng? *[Why not possible?]*

DAVID. Tā shì lǎo wài. Nǐ bù liǎo jiě tā. *[He's a foreigner. You don't even know him.]*

XIAO MEI. Wǒ yīng gāi zhī dào de zǎo jiù zhī dào le. *[I know what I need to know.]*

DAVID. Nà nǐ xū yào zhī dào shénme? *[Which is what?]*

XIAO MEI. Nǐ bù huì dǒng de, Dà Wéi. *[You wouldn't understand, Dà Wéi.]*

DAVID. Wǒ bù dǒng shì ma? *[I wouldn't understand, huh?]* *(holding up the bottle)* Zhù wǒ bù dǒng de shì, uh? Gān bēi! *[To whatever I don't understand, huh? Cheers!]*

SCENE 11

(The hotel room)

*(**MALCOLM***'s duffel bag is open on the bed. He's been packing.)*

(he picks up the hotel phone, presses a button, waits)

MALCOLM. Hello…? Nǐ hǎo. Uh…Any – messages for…? No, that's – Um. Wǒ xū yào yí liàng chū zū chē *[I need a taxi]*. To the airport?

(beat)

Hǎo de. Xiè xie nǐ. *[Great. Thanks.]*

(he hangs up the phone, glances at his watch)

*(he opens an envelope, takes out **XIAO MEI***'s red passport, flips through the pages)*

(he picks up his own blue passport from the bedside table, stows them both together in his money belt)

(He looks around the room, checking to see if he's forgotten anything.)

(There's a quiet knock at the door.)

MALCOLM. Finally…We gotta get –

(He opens the door.)

*(**DAVID** stands there, his suit dishevelled from a night of drinking.)*

(He's sober now, more or less, but mean and hungover.)

DAVID. Hey –

MALCOLM. Wang…

DAVID. Zěnmeyàng *[What's up]*, man…what's up?

*(he pushes past **MALCOLM** into the room)*

You expecting company?

MALCOLM. Yeah. In a minute, but –

DAVID. *(re: the duffel bag)* Going on a trip, huh?

MALCOLM. Like I told you...I have to leave for a while, before I can –

DAVID. Yeah, you could have just gone to Hong Kong, Malcolm. Don't have to fly halfway around the world, just to –

MALCOLM. I'm homesick, Wang.

DAVID. So you're not coming back?

MALCOLM. I don't know yet.

DAVID. What about my two weeks' notice? *(beat)* I'm kidding! I'm just fucking with you, man. Where is she?

MALCOLM. She's on her way.

DAVID. Oh yeah?

> *(beat)*

> So...got your own guānxi *[connections]* now, uh? Old China hand? Got a visa yourself? Don't need my help no more...

MALCOLM. No, I'm glad you're here, Wang. Actually. Because I wanted to say...in person, before we go, how much everything you've done has meant to –

DAVID. Oh, méi shì, méi shì. *[It's nothing, it's nothing.]*

MALCOLM. It's not nothing. Let me say this, all right? You've been a godsend for me...saved my life, bringing me to China. Got me this job. Place to stay. A girlfriend. When I was – unemployed and living out of my car, Wang. When I had nothing going on, back home –

DAVID. *(rhymes more with "bong")* It's Wang.

MALCOLM. Hm?

DAVID. Wang, Malcolm. Not "Wang." Fucking Wang, all right?

> *(beat)*

MALCOLM. Yeah, my bad...you didn't say anything, I thought –

DAVID. Because you don't listen.

(He takes a piece of folded paper from his jacket pocket.)

DAVID. Here – I want to show you something.

MALCOLM. What is it?

DAVID. Just a final Chinese lesson. Little parting gift.

(MALCOLM *takes the paper and unfolds it.)*

(It's a form, filled out completely in Chinese.)

MALCOLM. I can't read this...

DAVID. *(taking it back)* Here. I'll read it for you. It's a job application and work unit agreement. Between Xiao Mei and the People's Placement Corporation of Beijing. Lists her prior work experience. None. Professional references. None. Salary requirements. Any. Career goals: "Meet people. Work hard. Travel. Study my English." *(laughs, turns the paper over)* And it outlines our agreement. In exchange for receipt of residency forms, work permits, etc. The undersigned agrees to a three-year work contract with an employer designated by the PPCB...

MALCOLM. *(he'd already guessed)* She's one of your nóng nú. *[indentured servants.]*

DAVID. "Nóng nú"? That's a big word for you, Zhōng guó tōng. *[Old China hand.]* Where'd you learn that? Studying Chairman Mao?

MALCOLM. It doesn't matter. You can't enforce it. We're leaving –

DAVID. I'm not trying to enforce it, Malcolm. I'm trying to explain something to you...

MALCOLM. I get it. She works for you. So?

DAVID. Works for me? No, I'm just the middleman here... she works for you. She wanted to meet a foreigner. I introduced her to some possible employment opportunities. That's all. And you weren't the first, either.

(beat)

MALCOLM. She's never taken money –

DAVID. Not about money. She could have plenty of Chinese boyfriends these days with more money than you...she looks at you, she sees a way out.

MALCOLM. It's not like that...

DAVID. No? Look at yourself, Malcolm. You're the one who said she's out of your league, right? So what do you think closed the deal? Your hilarious lǎo wài *[foreigner]* sense of humor? Your natural way with the ladies? Bon Jovi? Come on, man...I told you what was going on, remember? That being lǎo wài *[foreign]* here gave you a leg up. That your American passport was a powerful aphrodisiac. I explained it to you, step by step. And you went and took advantage. So don't play the ignorant fucking tourist now!

MALCOLM. That's not the same as – I never asked – to be supplied with some geisha!

DAVID. Geishas are Japanese.

(there's a knock at the door)

*(After a moment, **MALCOLM** goes over and opens it.)*

*(**XIAO MEI** stands in the hallway, dressed for travel, pulling her roller bag.)*

XIAO MEI. Hi...

(they kiss briefly)

So sorry I am late, Mal-colm. Terrible traffic on Third Ring Road, I –

*(she notices **DAVID**, stops)*

DAVID. Zěnmeyàng, xiǎo jiě? *[How you doing, Miss?]* Long time no see...

(beat)

XIAO MEI. Nǐ hǎo *[hello]*, Dà Wéi...

*(**DAVID** folds up the piece of paper and tucks it back in his jacket pocket.)*

DAVID. Well. Feel like a third wheel on a flying pigeon. I should get going...nǐmen yào tán de shì háiyǒu hěn duō. *[You have a lot to catch up on.]*

(he goes to the door)

DAVID. Hey, gōng xǐ nǐ men *[congratulations]*, huh? Both of you. I'm really happy for you.

(he exits)

(beat)

*(**MALCOLM** turns, zips up his duffel bag)*

XIAO MEI. *(sensing something wrong)* Hey, Mal-colm. You o-kay...?

MALCOLM. Me? Yeah...I'm great. Why do you –

(She goes up to him, puts her hand on his chest)

XIAO MEI. Zěn me le? *[What's wrong?]*

MALCOLM. Nothing, just –

XIAO MEI. Nǐ zhēn de méi shì? *[Are you sure?]*

(beat)

MALCOLM. I have herpes.

XIAO MEI. Shénme...? *[What...?]*

MALCOLM. I'm sorry. I wanted to tell you before, it's – really a long story, but – Méi dú. *[Herpes.]* I have – Méi dú.

XIAO MEI. I know this. Already, Mal-colm...

MALCOLM. He told you...?

XIAO MEI. No. No, I find this – name of medicine on-line. Wal-trex? I think, you try to tell me, duì ma? *[yeah?]* Ask Dà Wéi for this translation, and he refuse?

MALCOLM. *(Nods)*

XIAO MEI. Mis-understanding, Mal-colm. Small thing between us now.

MALCOLM. You think so?

XIAO MEI. Yes, I think – *(checks her watch)* Maybe – it's good we leave at least one hour to get to Capital Airport...?

MALCOLM. Yeah.

(beat)

Um…there's something else, though, Mei – isn't there?

XIAO MEI. Shénme? [What is it?]

MALCOLM. I uh – (looks at her for a long time) There was – a little problem, it turns out. With the visa…I couldn't –

XIAO MEI. Zěn me le? [What?]

(he takes out her passport)

MALCOLM. Some kind of – hang-up. I don't know…

XIAO MEI. Fāshēng shénme shì le? [What happened?]

(he holds out the passport to her)

MALCOLM. I'm sorry. Nǐ tīng dǒng? [Understand?] But – I can't help you. In that way. So…if that's what you were looking for. From me, Xiao Mei – I can't –

XIAO MEI. I never say I want this, Mal-colm…this your idea, to have me see your hometown. Not mine.

MALCOLM. Yeah. So what is this then?

XIAO MEI. What is…?

MALCOLM. You work – for Wang? For Dà Wéi?

XIAO MEI. Yes?

MALCOLM. So this – is your job then? This?

XIAO MEI. No, not in the way you mean, Mal-colm…

MALCOLM. No? In what way then?

XIAO MEI. "What way"?

MALCOLM. What's the – arrangement here? How does it work?

XIAO MEI. To be – tour guide? And for Chinese lesson. Not for –

MALCOLM. No?

(the hotel phone rings)

(MALCOLM hesitates, and then picks up.)

MALCOLM. Wèi…? Hǎo. [Yes…? Okay.] I'll be right – Um… Yeah. Liǎng fēn zhōng [Two minutes], okay?

(he hangs up)

(They look at each other.)

XIAO MEI. Mal-colm...you think –

MALCOLM. Explain it to me. Please. I just need –

XIAO MEI. Explain – which?

MALCOLM. Everything. All of it. Okay? I'm trying to – this whole thing, Mei...I can't –

XIAO MEI. I – don't know how I –

MALCOLM. How – do you think about me? You know? How – does this feel? To you? I mean, am I – taking advantage? In some way, or – what is it? With us? Are we – using each other here...? Do we know each other at all? I can't quite –

(they look at each other helplessly)

(she approaches him, takes his face in her hands)

XIAO MEI. Hey – Mal-colm...

(long beat)

(They stare into each other's eyes.)

MALCOLM. Yeah, I – *(he pulls away)* Sorry, I just – I can't –

(he shoulders his bag, crosses to the door, hesitates, like he's about to say something else)

(And then he shakes his head, turns and exits, shutting the door quietly behind him.)

*(**XIAO MEI** stands there, alone.)*

(She sees her passport on the bed, picks it up, looks at it.)

(lights down)

End of Play

ACKNOWLEDGEMENTS

I wrote Outside People in Juilliard's American Playwrights Program, and the play is deeply indebted to the mentorship of Marsha Norman and Chris Durang, and to the other brilliant writers in the room: Andrea Ciannavei, Katori Hall, Sam Hunter, Nathan Jackson, Greg Keller, Molly Smith Metzler, Marco Ramirez, and Emily Schwend. I also benefited from the big brains of Sam Gold and Joe Kraemer, who brought their formidable talents to early workshops and conversations.

Evan Cabnet was a prodigy of a director—a passionate advocate, an insightful dramaturg, and an artistic genius. His cast—Matt Delapina, Nelson Lee, Li Jun Li, and Sonequa Martin-Green—created characters who spoke beautifully across languages, and his design team—Takeshi Kata, Ben Stanton, Jill B C Du Boff, and Jessica Wegener Shay—conjured an entire other world.

Doug Aibel produced the plays that first made me want to become a playwright, and it was a great honor to work in his theater. Andy Donald championed the play from the beginning, and he and Sarah Stern brought it to life with their brilliant and bold leadership; that they are the next generation of Artistic Directors gives me faith in the future of American theatre. Phyllis Wender supported this play, as she does all my work, with ferocity, integrity, wit, and warmth. I feel grateful to have her in my corner.

I learned about the Mandarin language and Chinese culture from Jo Mei, Jane Chen, Han Tang, James Chen, Da Ming Chen, Alex Jia, Jean Chen and especially my lifelong zhong guo tong tour guides: Ken, Judith, Jacob, and Aaron DeWoskin.

And finally, I could never have written "Foreign Guy in Beijing" without the inspiration of my own yang niu, Rachel DeWoskin, who translates the world for me.

Lightning Source UK Ltd.
Milton Keynes UK
UKOW04f1504230714

235640UK00001B/11/P